Introducing Famous Americans

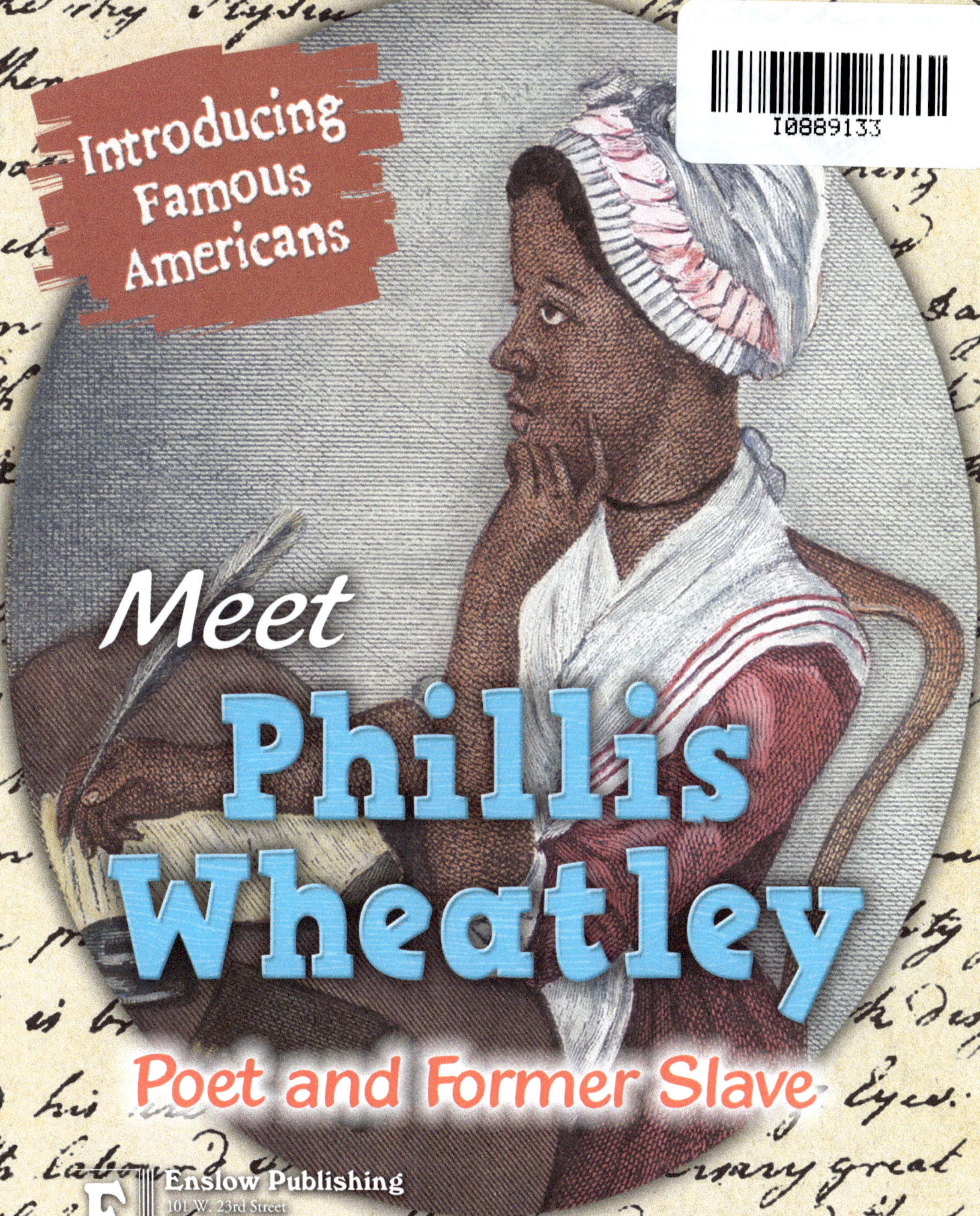

Meet Phillis Wheatley

Poet and Former Slave

Enslow Publishing
101 W. 23rd Street
Suite 240
New York, NY 10011
USA
enslow.com

Jane Katirgis and J. T. Moriarty

Published in 2020 by Enslow Publishing, LLC
101 W. 23rd Street, Suite 240, New York, NY 10011

Library of Congress Cataloging-in-Publication Data

Names: Katirgis, Jane, author. | Moriarty, J. T., author.
Title: Meet Phillis Wheatley : poet and former slave / Jane Katirgis and J. T. Moriarty.
Description: New York : Enslow Publishing, 2020. | Series: Introducing famous Americans | Audience: Grades 3–5. | Includes bibliographical references and index.
Identifiers: LCCN 2018060044| ISBN 9781978511286 (library bound) | ISBN 9781978511262 (paperback) | ISBN 9781978511279 (6 pack)
Subjects: LCSH: Wheatley, Phillis, 1753–1784—Juvenile literature. | African American women poets—Biography—Juvenile literature. | Women slaves—United States—Biography—Juvenile literature.
Classification: LCC PS866.W5 Z634 2019 | DDC 811/.1 [B]—dc23
LC record available at https://lccn.loc.gov/2018060044

Printed in the United States of America

To Our Readers: We have done our best to make sure all website addresses in this book were active and appropriate when we went to press. However, the author and the publisher have no control over and assume no liability for the material available on those websites or on any websites they may link to. Any comments or suggestions can be sent by email to customerservice@enslow.com.

Portions of this book originally appeared in *Phillis Wheatley: African American Poet.*

Photo Credits: Cover, p. 1 (Wheatley), pp. 8, 21, 23 Bettmann/Getty Images; cover, p. 1 (script) Nina_Susik/Shutterstock.com; p. 4 Library of Congress Geography and Map Division; p. 5 Library of Congress/Corbis Historical/Getty Images; p. 7 © North Wind Picture Archives; p. 9 3LH/SuperStock; pp. 10, 18 Library of Congress Rare Book and Special Collections Division; p. 11 The Library Company of Philadelphia; p. 13 Collection of the Massachusetts Historical Society; pp. 14, 17 (top) De Agostini Picture Library/Getty Images; p. 15 Library of Congress Manuscript Division; p. 17 (bottom) From *The poems of Phillis Wheatley, as they were originally published in London*, 1773, by Phillis Wheatley (Philadelphia, 1909)/Internet Archive/CC0; p. 19 Francis G. Mayer/Corbis Historical/Getty Images; p. 22 Schomburg Center, NYPL/Art Resource, NY; p. 24 Library of Congress Printed Ephemera Collection; p. 26 From the *Independent Chronicle and Universal Advertiser*, Boston, MA, Dec. 9, 1784. Image courtesy of the Rare Books and Manuscripts Collection, The New York Public Library, Astor, Lenox, and Tilden Foundations; interior pages background pattern and graphic elements Ambient Ideas/Shutterstock.com.

Contents

1 Sold into Slavery

Hundreds of years ago, the world was a different place. The year was 1761. White men sailed to Africa. They took African people from their homes. They forced a girl about seven years old into a ship. It was packed with other African people who had been kidnapped. There were men and women, boys and girls.

This map of Africa was drawn in 1725. The slave ship to Boston that Phillis was carried on was returning from the west coast of Africa.

The boat sailed across the Middle Passage. This was a route used by slave ships to travel from Africa to America.

The conditions on the ship were terrible. The Africans were tightly packed together. It was dark and hot. The African people wore heavy chains. They could not move very much. They didn't have much to eat or drink.

Many people imprisoned on slave ships got sick and died. The trip from Africa took months.

The ship finally reached Boston. The young girl was sold at a slave auction. She was very weak. All she wore was a piece of dirty carpet. She was missing two front teeth.

The Wheatley family bought her. They did not know her name. She could not tell them. She did not speak English. They named her Phillis. It was the name of the slave ship.

Let's Learn More

Phillis arrived in Boston on July 11, 1761.

Let's Learn More

The Wheatley children were twins. Their names were Mary and Nathaniel.

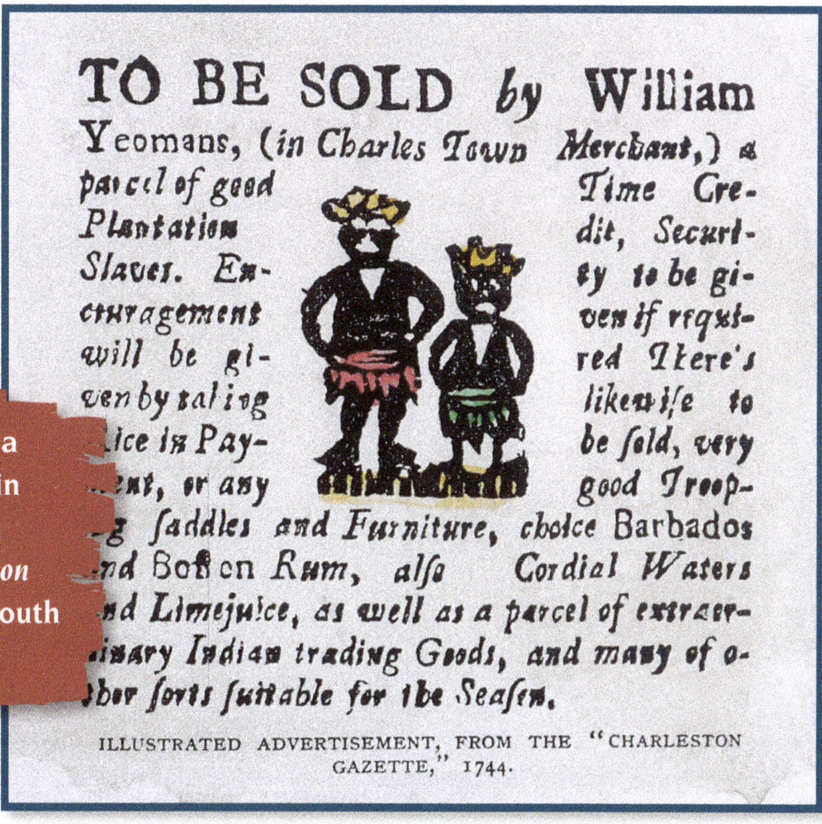

This ad for a slave sale in 1744 ran in the *Charleston Gazette* in South Carolina.

Phillis was too sick to work hard in the house. But she was very smart. Mary Wheatley taught Phillis to speak English. She taught Phillis to read and write English, too. She also taught her to read Latin. Phillis worked very hard at her lessons. Soon she could read the Bible. Mrs. Wheatley was very happy to see Phillis learn so quickly.

Phillis learned to read, perhaps with a book like this.

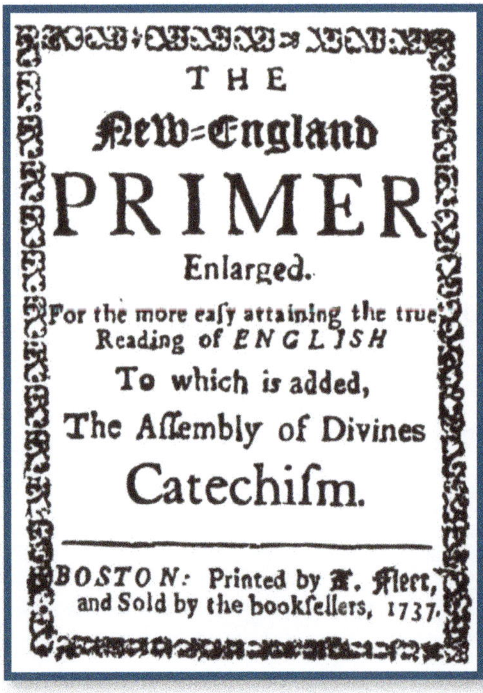
THE

New-England

PRIMER

Enlarged.

For the more eaſy attaining the true Reading of ENGLISH

To which is added,

The Aſſembly of Divines

Catechiſm.

BOSTON: Printed by T. Fleet, and Sold by the bookſellers, 1737.

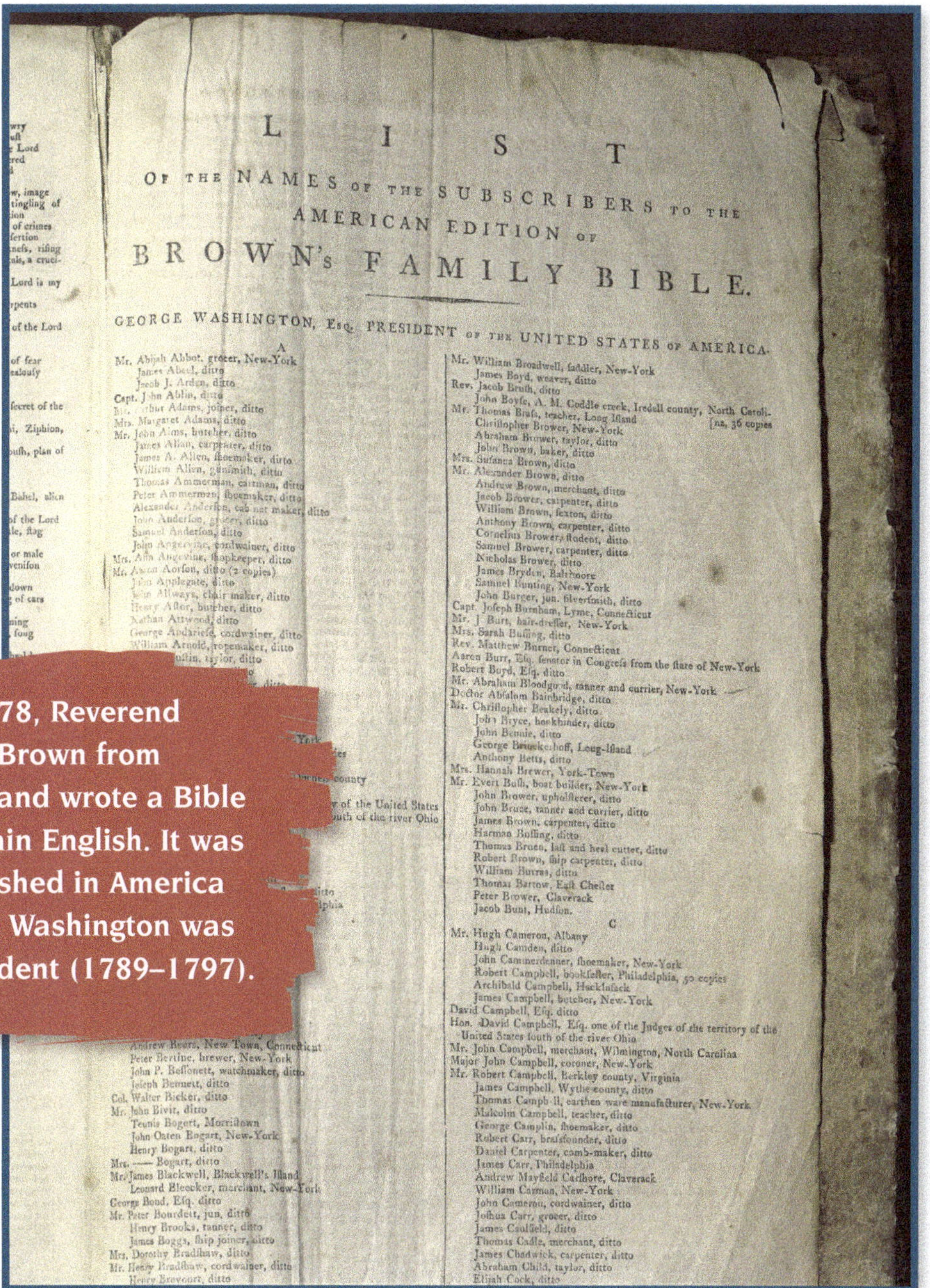

LIST
OF THE NAMES OF THE SUBSCRIBERS TO THE AMERICAN EDITION OF
BROWN's FAMILY BIBLE.

GEORGE WASHINGTON, Esq. PRESIDENT OF THE UNITED STATES OF AMERICA.

A

Mr. Abijah Abbot, grocer, New-York
James Abeel, ditto
Jacob J. Arden, ditto
Capt. John Ablin, ditto
Mrs. Margaret Adams, ditto
Mr. John Aims, butcher, ditto
James Allan, carpenter, ditto
James A. Allen, shoemaker, ditto
William Allen, gunsmith, ditto
Thomas Ammerman, cartman, ditto
Peter Ammerman, shoemaker, ditto
Alexander Anderson, cabinet maker, ditto
John Anderson, grocer, ditto
Samuel Anderson, ditto
John Angevine, cordwainer, ditto
Mrs. Ann Angevine, shopkeeper, ditto
Mr. Aaron Aorson, ditto (2 copies)
John Applegate, ditto
John Allways, chair maker, ditto
Henry Astor, butcher, ditto
Nathan Attwood, ditto
George Andariese, cordwainer, ditto
William Arnold, ropemaker, ditto

Andrew Beers, New Town, Connecticut
Peter Bertine, brewer, New-York
John P. Bessonett, watchmaker, ditto
Joseph Bennett, ditto
Col. Walter Bicker, ditto
Mr. John Bivit, ditto
Teunis Bogert, Morristown
John Oaten Bogart, New-York
Henry Bogart, ditto
Mrs. —— Bogart, ditto
Mr. James Blackwell, Blackwell's Island
Leonard Bleecker, merchant, New-York
George Bond, Esq. ditto
Mr. Peter Bourdett, jun. ditto
Henry Brooks, tanner, ditto
James Boggs, ship joiner, ditto
Mrs. Dorothy Bradshaw, ditto
Mr. Henry Bradshaw, cordwainer, ditto
Henry Brevoort, ditto

Mr. William Broadwell, saddler, New-York
James Boyd, weaver, ditto
Rev. Jacob Brush, ditto
John Boyse, A. M. Coddle creek, Iredell county, North Carolina, 36 copies
Mr. Thomas Brass, teacher, Long Island
Christopher Brower, New-York
Abraham Brower, taylor, ditto
John Brown, baker, ditto
Mrs. Susanna Brown, ditto
Mr. Alexander Brown, ditto
Andrew Brown, merchant, ditto
Jacob Brower, carpenter, ditto
William Brown, sexton, ditto
Anthony Brown, carpenter, ditto
Cornelius Brower, student, ditto
Samuel Brower, carpenter, ditto
Nicholas Brower, ditto
James Bryden, Baltimore
Samuel Bunting, New-York
John Burger, jun. silversmith, ditto
Capt. Joseph Burnham, Lyme, Connecticut
Mr. J. Burt, hair-dresser, New-York
Mrs. Sarah Bussing, ditto
Rev. Matthew Burnet, Connecticut
Aaron Burr, Esq. senator in Congress from the state of New-York
Robert Boyd, Esq. ditto
Mr. Abraham Bloodgood, tanner and currier, New-York
Doctor Absalom Bainbridge, ditto
Mr. Christopher Beakely, ditto
John Bryce, bookbinder, ditto
John Bennie, ditto
George Brinckerhoff, Long-Island
Anthony Betts, ditto
Mrs. Hannah Brewer, York-Town
Mr. Evert Bush, boat builder, New-York
John Brower, upholsterer, ditto
John Bruce, tanner and currier, ditto
James Brown, carpenter, ditto
Harmon Bussing, ditto
Thomas Bruen, last and heel cutter, ditto
Robert Brown, ship carpenter, ditto
William Burras, ditto
Thomas Barrow, East Chester
Peter Brower, Claverack
Jacob Bunt, Hudson.

C

Mr. Hugh Cameron, Albany
Hugh Camden, ditto
John Cammerdenner, shoemaker, New-York
Robert Campbell, bookseller, Philadelphia, 50 copies
Archibald Campbell, Hackinsack
James Campbell, butcher, New-York
David Campbell, Esq. ditto
Hon. David Campbell, Esq. one of the Judges of the territory of the United States south of the river Ohio
Mr. John Campbell, merchant, Wilmington, North Carolina
Major John Campbell, coroner, New-York
Mr. Robert Campbell, Berkley county, Virginia
James Campbell, Wythe county, ditto
Thomas Campbell, earthen ware manufacturer, New-York
Malcolm Campbell, teacher, ditto
George Camplin, shoemaker, ditto
Robert Carr, brassfounder, ditto
Daniel Carpenter, comb-maker, ditto
James Carr, Philadelphia
Andrew Mayfield Carshore, Claverack
William Carman, New-York
John Cameron, cordwainer, ditto
Joshua Carr, grocer, ditto
James Caulfield, ditto
Thomas Cadle, merchant, ditto
James Chadwick, carpenter, ditto
Abraham Child, taylor, ditto
Elijah Cock, ditto

In 1778, Reverend John Brown from Scotland wrote a Bible in plain English. It was published in America while Washington was president (1789–1797).

2 Reading and Writing

At this time, most white people in America didn't understand African culture. Black people from Africa had a different way of life from white people in America. White people thought Africans were inferior. They treated African slaves like animals.

Many white people were impressed by Phillis. Because she could read and write, she was treated better than most slaves.

Young Phillis was best known for writing "On the Death of the Reverend George Whitefield, 1770." Reverend Whitefield had wanted to start a school for free blacks.

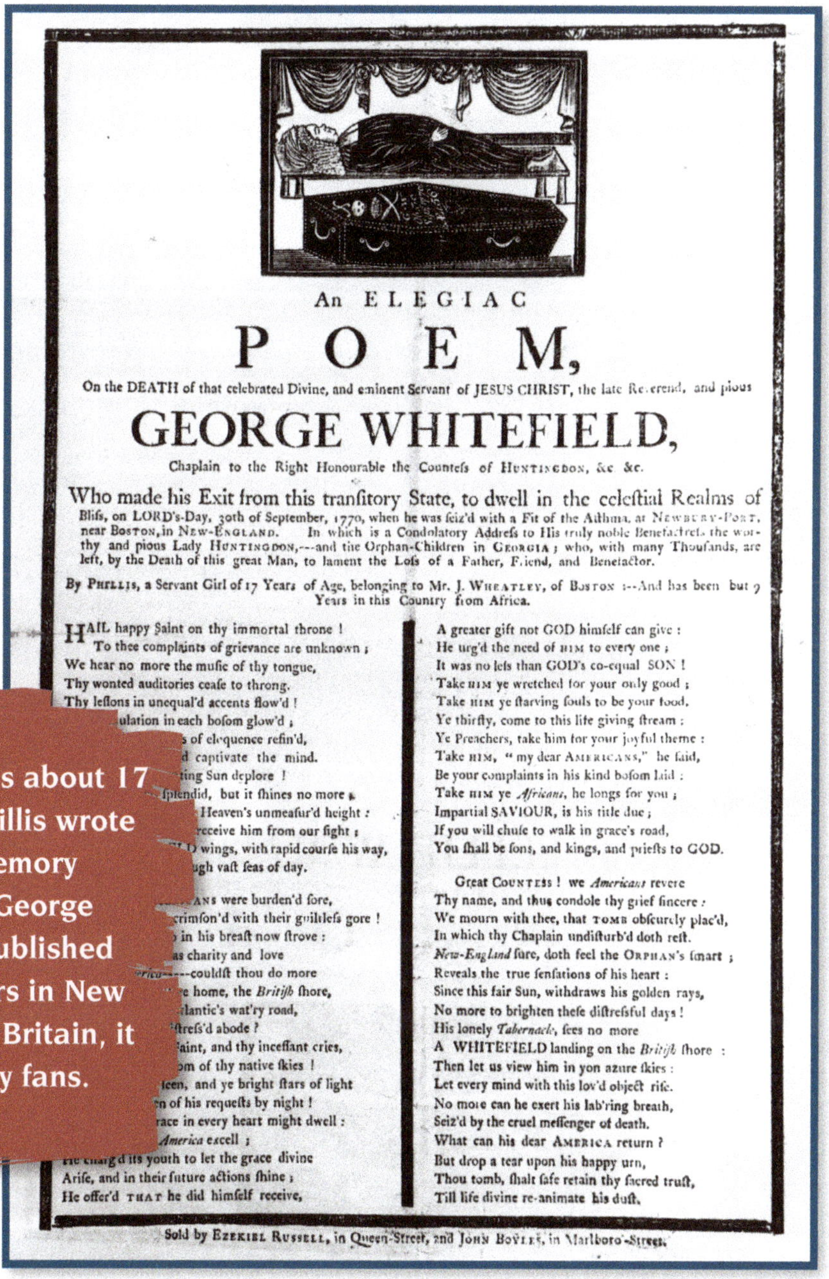
An ELEGIAC

POEM,

On the DEATH of that celebrated Divine, and eminent Servant of JESUS CHRIST, the late Reverend, and pious

GEORGE WHITEFIELD,

Chaplain to the Right Honourable the Countefs of HUNTINGDON, &c &c.

Who made his Exit from this tranfitory State, to dwell in the celeftial Realms of Blifs, on LORD's-Day, 30th of September, 1770, when he was feiz'd with a Fit of the Afthma, at NEWBURY-PORT, near BOSTON, in NEW-ENGLAND. In which is a Condolatory Addrefs to His truly noble Benefactrefs the worthy and pious Lady HUNTINGDON,---and the Orphan-Children in GEORGIA; who, with many Thoufands, are left, by the Death of this great Man, to lament the Lofs of a Father, Friend, and Benefactor.

By PHILLIS, a Servant Girl of 17 Years of Age, belonging to Mr. J. WHEATLEY, of BOSTON:--And has been but 9 Years in this Country from Africa.

HAIL happy Saint on thy immortal throne!
To thee complaints of grievance are unknown;
We hear no more the mufic of thy tongue,
Thy wonted auditories ceafe to throng.
Thy leffons in unequal'd accents flow'd!
...ulation in each bofom glow'd;
...s of eloquence refin'd,
...d captivate the mind.
...ting Sun deplore!
...fplendid, but it fhines no more.
... Heaven's unmeafur'd height:
...receive him from our fight;
...D wings, with rapid courfe his way,
...ugh vaft feas of day.

...ANS were burden'd fore,
...crimfon'd with their guiltlefs gore!
... in his breaft now ftrove:
...as charity and love
...rica----couldft thou do more
...e home, the *Britifh* fhore,
...lantic's wat'ry road,
...ftrefs'd abode?
...aint, and thy inceffant cries,
...om of thy native fkies!
...feen, and ye bright ftars of light
...n of his requefts by night!
...race in every heart might dwell:
... *America* excell;
...charg'd its youth to let the grace divine
Arife, and in their future actions fhine;
He offer'd THAT he did himfelf receive,
A greater gift not GOD himfelf can give:
He urg'd the need of HIM to every one;
It was no lefs than GOD's co-equal SON!
Take HIM ye wretched for your only good;
Take HIM ye ftarving fouls to be your food.
Ye thirfty, come to this life giving ftream:
Ye Preachers, take him for your joyful theme:
Take HIM, "my dear AMERICANS," he faid,
Be your complaints in his kind bofom laid:
Take HIM ye *Africans*, he longs for you;
Impartial SAVIOUR, is his title due;
If you will chufe to walk in grace's road,
You fhall be fons, and kings, and priefts to GOD.

Great COUNTESS! we *Americans* revere
Thy name, and thus condole thy grief fincere:
We mourn with thee, that TOMB obfcurely plac'd,
In which thy Chaplain undifturb'd doth reft.
New-England fure, doth feel the ORPHAN's fmart;
Reveals the true fenfations of his heart:
Since this fair Sun, withdraws his golden rays,
No more to brighten thefe diftrefsful days!
His lonely *Tabernacle*, fees no more
A WHITEFIELD landing on the *Britifh* fhore:
Then let us view him in yon azure fkies:
Let every mind with this lov'd object rife.
No more can he exert his lab'ring breath,
Seiz'd by the cruel meffenger of death.
What can his dear AMERICA return?
But drop a tear upon his happy urn,
Thou tomb, fhalt fafe retain thy facred truft,
Till life divine re-animate his duft.

Sold by EZEKIEL RUSSELL, in Queen-Street, and JOHN BOYLES, in Marlboro-Street.

When she was about 17 years old, Phillis wrote a poem in memory of Reverend George Whitefield. Published in newspapers in New England and Britain, it won her many fans.

Phillis soon began to write poetry. She wrote about religion. She wrote about people she met and things she saw. She wrote about famous people, like George Washington. Mrs. Wheatley liked her poetry. She encouraged Phillis to keep writing.

In some ways, the Wheatleys treated her like a member of the family. They were very proud of her. But she was still a slave.

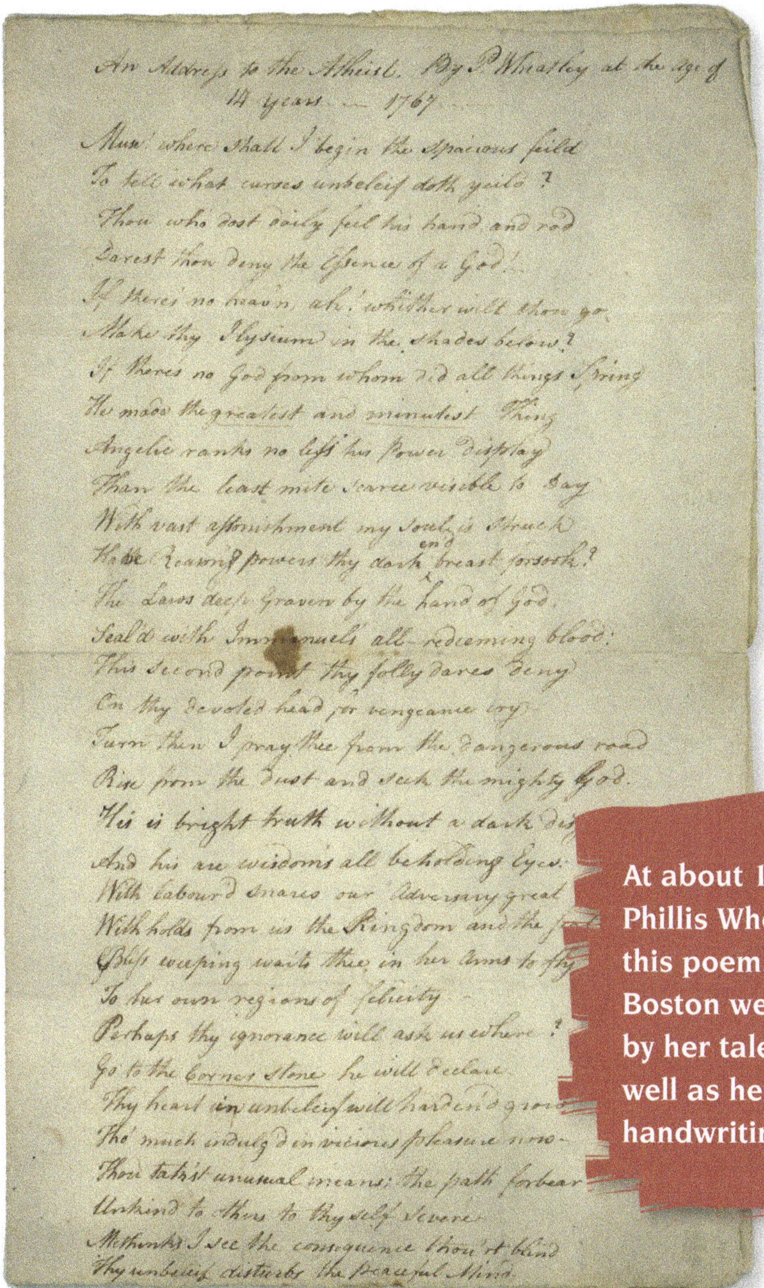

An Address to the Atheist. By P. Wheatley at the age of 14 years — 1767

Muse! where shall I begin the spacious feild
To tell what curses unbeleif doth yeild?
Thou who dost daily feel his hand and rod
Darest thou deny the Essence of a God!
If there's no heav'n, ah! whither wilt thou go
Make thy Ilysium in the shades below?
If there's no God from whom did all things Spring
He made the greatest and minutest Thing
Angelic ranks no less his Power display
Than the least mite scarce visible to Day
With vast astonishment my soul is struck
Have Reason's powers thy darken'd breast forsook?
The Laws deep Graven by the hand of God,
Seal'd with Immanuel's all-redeeming blood:
This second point thy folly dares deny
On thy devoted head for vengeance cry
Turn then I pray thee from the dangerous road
Rise from the dust and seek the mighty God.
His is bright truth without a dark dis
And his are wisdom's all beholding Eyes.
With labour'd snares our Adversary great
Withholds from us the Kingdom and the
Bliss weeping waits thee, in her Arms to fly
To her own regions of felicity
Perhaps thy ignorance will ask us where?
Go to the Corner stone he will declare.
Thy heart in unbeleif will harden'd grow
Tho' much indulg'd in vicious pleasure now—
Thou tak'st unusual means; the path forbear
Unkind to others to thyself severe
Methinks I see the consequence thou'rt blind
Thy unbeleif disturbs the peaceful Mind.

At about 14 years old, Phillis Wheatley wrote this poem. People in Boston were amazed by her talent, as well as her beautiful handwriting.

Many white people didn't believe Phillis could write poems. Most white people thought people with dark skin were not smart. Famous white people had written articles about black people. They said people with dark skin were a different species from white people.

David Hume, an important Scottish philosopher, was one of the people who did not believe that Phillis could have written her own poetry.

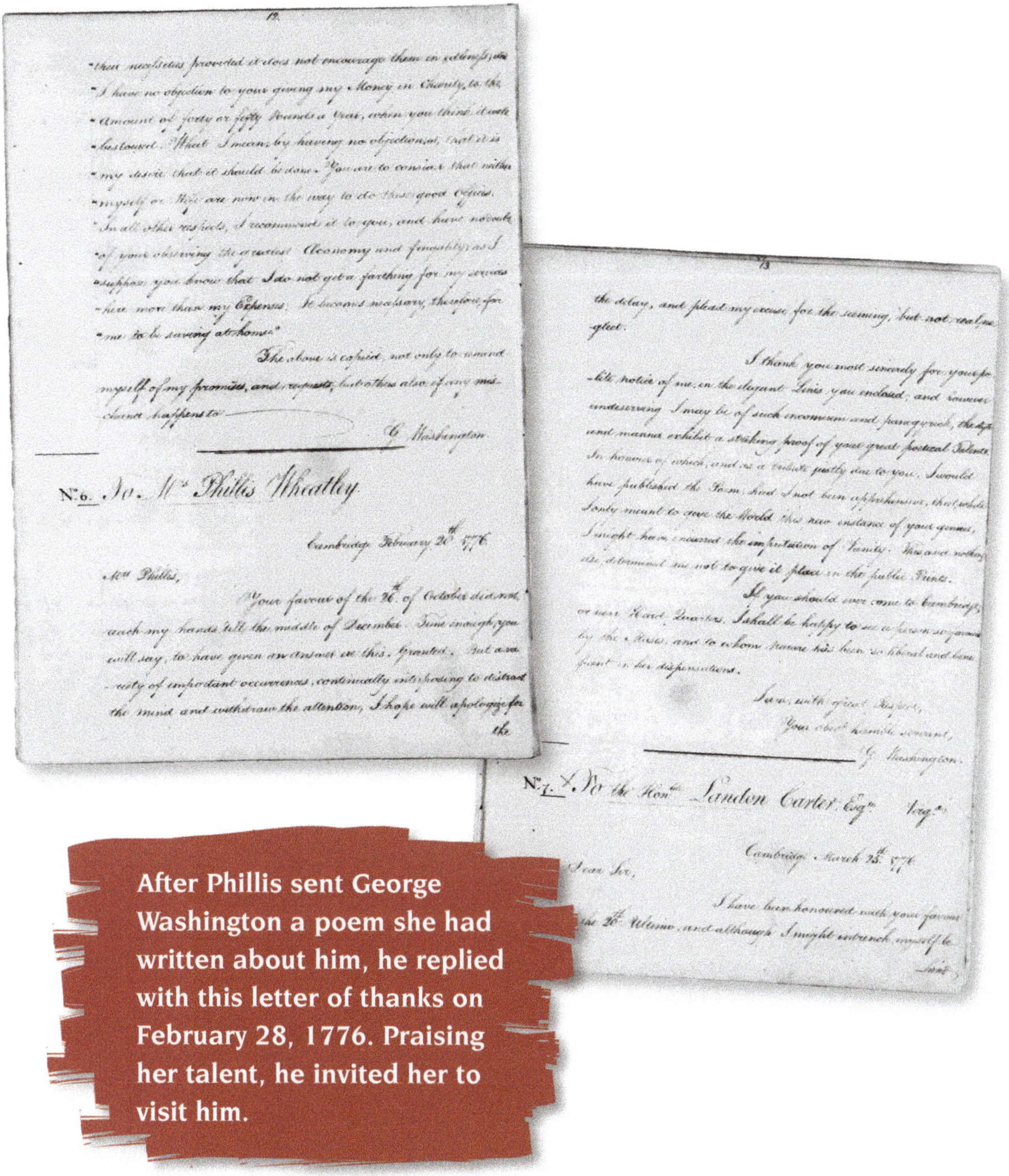

12

"their necessities provided it does not encourage them in idleness; and
"I have no objection to your giving my Money in Charity, to the
"amount of forty or fifty Pounds a Year, when you think it well
"bestowed. What I mean, by having no objection, is, that it is
"my desire that it should be done. You are to consider that neither
"myself or Wife are now in the way to do these good Offices.
"In all other respects, I recommend it to you, and have no doubt
"of your observing the greatest Economy and frugality; as I
"suppose you know that I do not get a farthing for my services
"here more than my Expenses. It becomes necessary, therefore, for
"me to be saving at home."

The above is copied, not only to remind myself of my promises, and requests, but others also if any mischance happens to

G. Washington

No. 6. To Mrs Phillis Wheatley

Cambridge February 28th 1776

Mrs Phillis,

Your favour of the 26th of October did not reach my hands till the middle of December. Time enough, you will say, to have given an answer ere this. Granted. But a variety of important occurrences, continually interposing to distract the mind and withdraw the attention, I hope will apologize for the

13

the delay, and plead my excuse for the seeming, but not real neglect.

I thank you most sincerely for your polite notice of me, in the elegant Lines you enclosed; and however undeserving I may be of such encomium and panegyrick, the style and manner exhibit a striking proof of your great poetical Talents. In honour of which, and as a tribute justly due to you, I would have published the Poem, had I not been apprehensive, that, while I only meant to give the World this new instance of your genius, I might have incurred the imputation of Vanity. This and nothing else, determined me not to give it place in the public Prints.

If you should ever come to Cambridge, or near Head Quarters, I shall be happy to see a person so favoured by the Muses, and to whom Nature has been so liberal and beneficent in her dispensations.

I am, with great Respect,
Your obedt humble servant,
G. Washington

No. 7. To the Honble Landon Carter Esqr.

Cambridge March 25th 1776

Dear Sir,

I have been honoured with your favour of the 20th Ultimo, and although I might intrench myself be

After Phillis sent George Washington a poem she had written about him, he replied with this letter of thanks on February 28, 1776. Praising her talent, he invited her to visit him.

Mr. Wheatley wanted to prove that Phillis was very smart. He wanted to show the world that she had written her own poems.

He arranged for a group of men in Boston to question Phillis. They included the governor of Massachusetts, John Hancock, and church leaders. They decided that her intelligence was real.

Let's Learn More

Many white people came to meet Phillis. To them, she was a living wonder. She was unusual to them because she was an African American who could read and write poetry.

Nearly all of the men who tested Phillis to see if she was really smart owned slaves. One of the men was John Hancock.

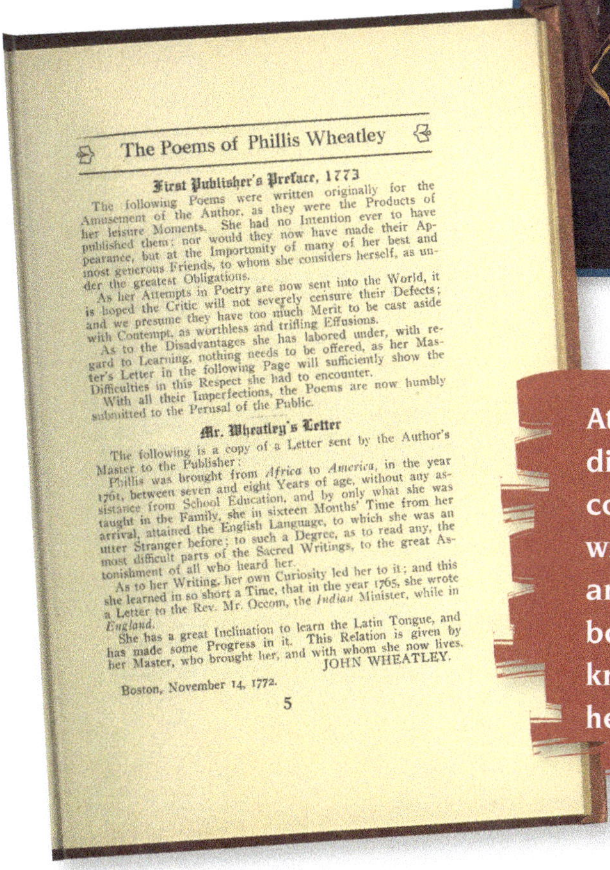

The Poems of Phillis Wheatley

First Publisher's Preface, 1773

The following Poems were written originally for the
Amusement of the Author, as they were the Products of
her leisure Moments. She had no Intention ever to have
published them; nor would they now have made their Ap-
pearance, but at the Importunity of many of her best and
most generous Friends, to whom she considers herself, as un-
der the greatest Obligations.
As her Attempts in Poetry are now sent into the World, it
is hoped the Critic will not severely censure their Defects;
and we presume they have too much Merit to be cast aside
with Contempt, as worthless and trifling Effusions.
As to the Disadvantages she has labored under, with re-
gard to Learning, nothing needs to be offered, as her Mas-
ter's Letter in the following Page will sufficiently show the
Difficulties in this Respect she had to encounter.
With all their Imperfections, the Poems are now humbly
submitted to the Perusal of the Public.

Mr. Wheatley's Letter

The following is a copy of a Letter sent by the Author's
Master to the Publisher:
Phillis was brought from *Africa* to *America*, in the year
1761, between seven and eight Years of age, without any as-
sistance from School Education, and by only what she was
taught in the Family, she in sixteen Months' Time from her
arrival, attained the English Language, to which she was an
utter Stranger before; to such a Degree, as to read any, the
most difficult parts of the Sacred Writings, to the great As-
tonishment of all who heard her.
As to her Writing, her own Curiosity led her to it; and this
she learned in so short a Time, that in the year 1765, she wrote
a Letter to the Rev. Mr. Occom, the *Indian* Minister, while in
England.
She has a great Inclination to learn the Latin Tongue, and
has made some Progress in it. This Relation is given by
her Master, who brought her, and with whom she now lives.

JOHN WHEATLEY.

Boston, November 14, 1772.

5

At the time, many people did not believe that Africans could learn to read and write. John Wheatley wrote an introduction to Phillis's book. He wanted people to know she had really written her own poems.

At that time, Massachusetts was a British colony. Many colonists were unhappy with British rules. They did not want to pay taxes to Great Britain for tea and other things. These colonists were ready to fight for freedom from Britain. The American Revolution was coming. Phillis would see what was happening from her home in Boston.

The Boston Tea Party took place near where Phillis lived in 1773.

The Battle of Bunker Hill was the first major battle of the Revolutionary War. It took place near Boston in 1775. It proved that Americans could put up a good fight against the British.

3 Phillis Writes a Book of Poetry

Phillis was a talented writer and wrote many poems. Mrs. Wheatley arranged for them to be published. Phillis wrote a book. No one in Boston would publish it because it was written by a slave.

The Wheatleys sent a copy of Phillis's book to London. Archibald Bell agreed to publish it there. The book would have a picture of Phillis in it. People would know she was black.

Let's Learn More

It is believed that the slave Scipio Moorhead drew the portrait of Phillis for her book.

Phillis's book was being published in London. She and Mr. Wheatley sailed there. The sea air was good for her asthma.

Phillis met many celebrities in London. Even King George wanted to meet her.

When Phillis and Mr. Wheatley returned to Boston, the Wheatleys freed her. She was no longer a slave!

Phillis Wheatley's book was published in 1773. It was the first book of poetry written by an African American woman. Her portrait appeared on the first page of her book.

This is a rare picture of Phillis Wheatley dressed in a gown and jewels. It appeared in a French magazine between 1834 and 1842.

Let's Learn More

Anne Bradstreet was the first American woman poet to be published. Phillis was the second.

4 A Later Life of Struggle

In just a few short years, Phillis's life got much harder. All the Wheatleys, who had helped her so much, had died.

John Peters was another freed slave. Phillis married him in 1778. John struggled to make ends meet. They sank into terrible poverty. Phillis's three children died. John abandoned her. Some historians think he went to debtor's prison.

This is what a prison looked like in 1809. In the 1700s, people who could not pay their bills were sent to debtor's prison.

Phillis wrote many letters. We know a lot about her because many people saved the letters.

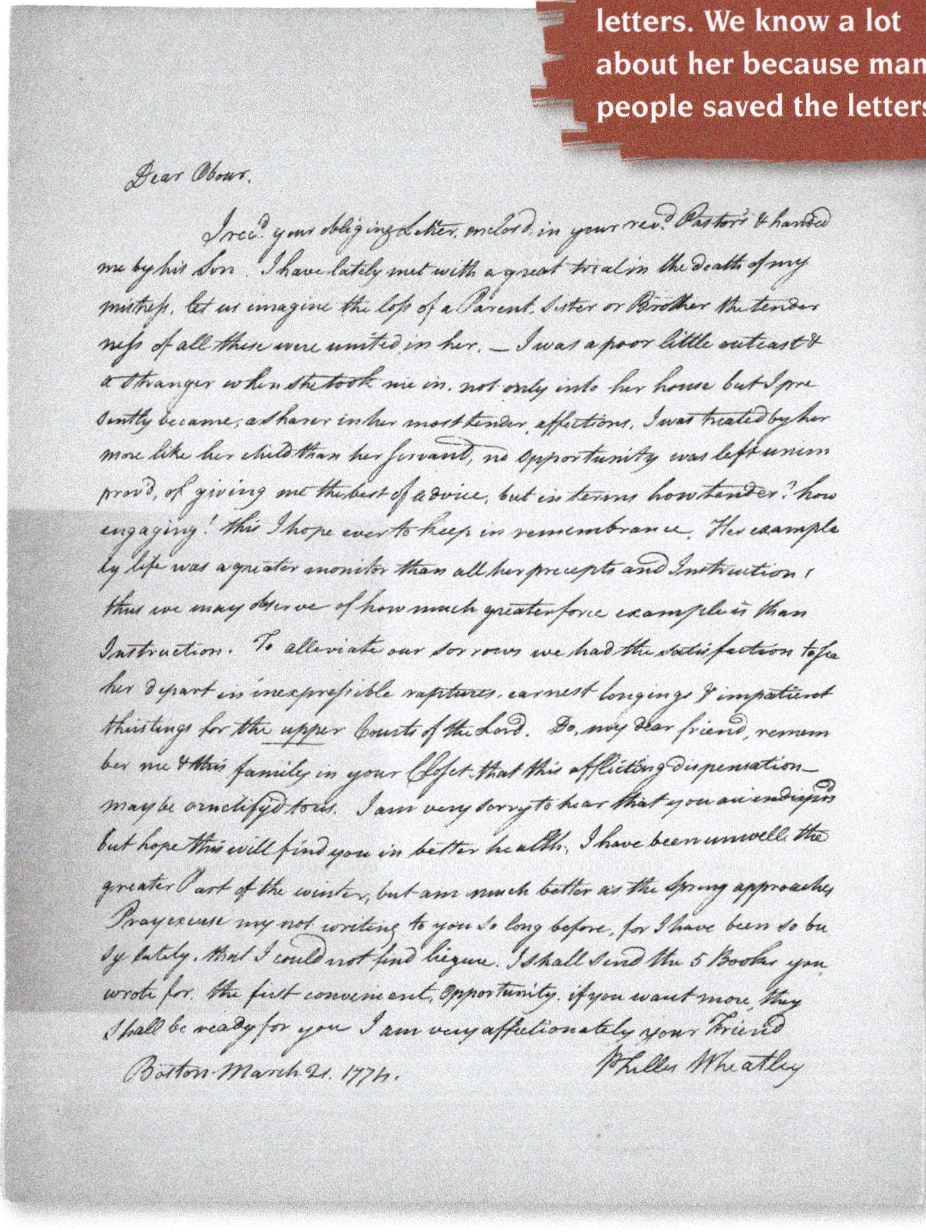

Dear Obour,

I rec'd your obliging Letter, enclos'd, in your revd Pastor's & handed me by his Son. I have lately met with a great trial in the death of my mistress; let us imagine the loss of a Parent, Sister or Brother the tenderness of all these were united in her. — I was a poor little outcast & a Stranger when she took me in: not only into her house but I presently became a sharer in her most tender affections. I was treated by her more like her child than her servant; no Opportunity was left unimprov'd, of giving me the best of advice, but in terms how tender! how engaging! this I hope ever to keep in remembrance. Her example by life was a greater monitor than all her precepts and Instruction; thus we may observe of how much greater force example is than Instruction. To alleviate our sorrows we had the satisfaction to see her depart in inexpressible raptures, earnest longings & impatient thirstings for the upper Courts of the Lord. Do, my dear friend, remember me & this family in your Closet, that this afflicting dispensation may be sanctify'd to us. I am very sorry to hear that you are indispos'd but hope this will find you in better health. I have been unwell the greater Part of the winter, but am much better as the Spring approaches. Pray excuse my not writing to you so long before, for I have been so busy lately, that I could not find leisure. I shall send the 5 Books you wrote for, the first convenient Opportunity; if you want more, they shall be ready for you. I am very affectionately your Friend

Boston March 21. 1774.

Phillis Wheatley

Phillis became very poor. She could not sell another book.

She died in 1784, at the age of thirty-one. Nobody knows for sure where she is buried.

Fifty years later, Margaretta Odell wrote a book about Phillis. It was very sad. Being black in a white society took its toll. Phillis was brave. We should remember her struggle.

Let's Learn More

In 1998 a poem called "Ocean" by Phillis Wheatley was discovered in an attic. It sold for almost $70,000.

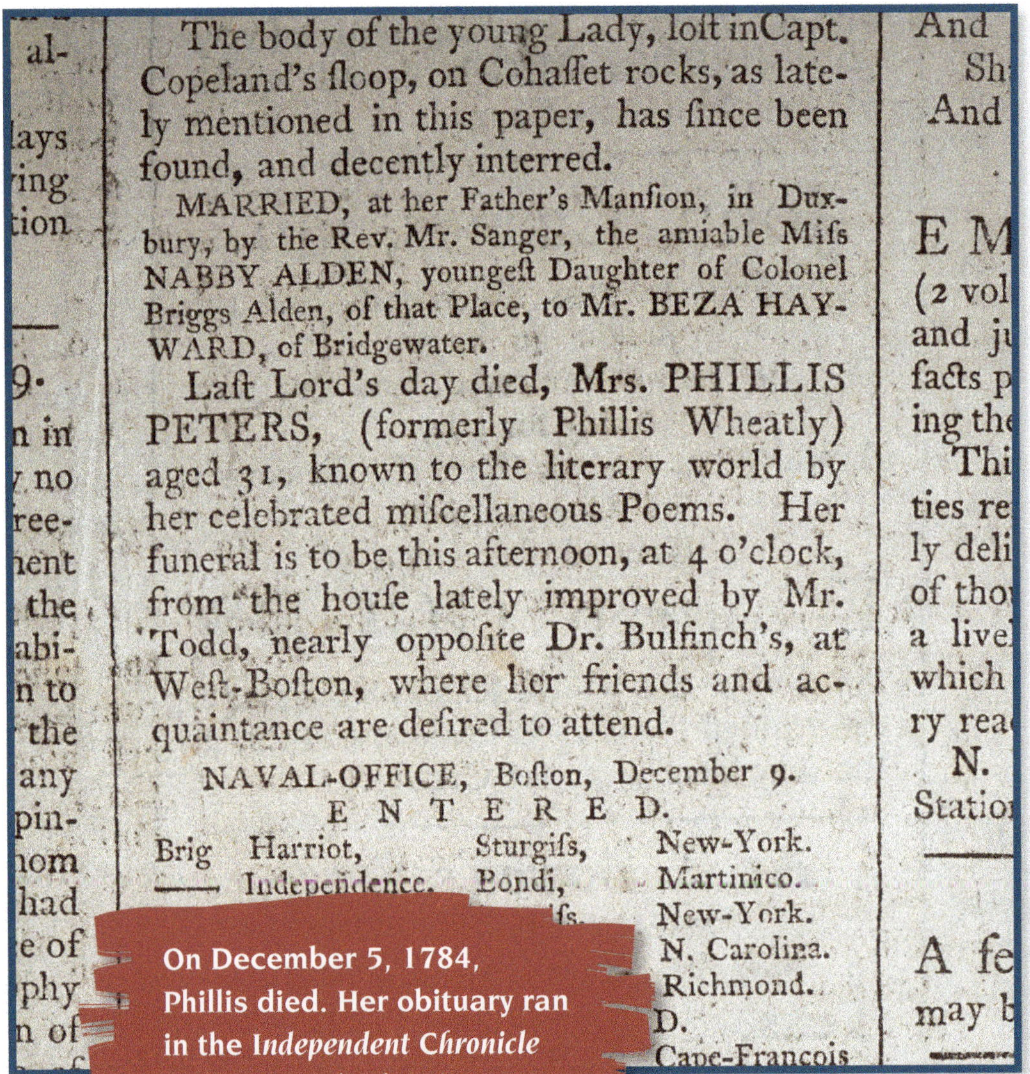

The body of the young Lady, loſt in Capt. Copeland's ſloop, on Cohaſſet rocks, as lately mentioned in this paper, has ſince been found, and decently interred.

MARRIED, at her Father's Manſion, in Duxbury, by the Rev. Mr. Sanger, the amiable Miſs NABBY ALDEN, youngeſt Daughter of Colonel Briggs Alden, of that Place, to Mr. BEZA HAYWARD, of Bridgewater.

Laſt Lord's day died, Mrs. PHILLIS PETERS, (formerly Phillis Wheatly) aged 31, known to the literary world by her celebrated miſcellaneous Poems. Her funeral is to be this afternoon, at 4 o'clock, from the houſe lately improved by Mr. Todd, nearly oppoſite Dr. Bulfinch's, at Weſt-Boſton, where her friends and acquaintance are deſired to attend.

NAVAL-OFFICE, Boſton, December 9.

E N T E R E D.

Brig Harriot, Sturgiſs, New-York.
—— Independence, Bondi, Martinico.
New-York.
N. Carolina.
Richmond.
D.
Cape-Francois

On December 5, 1784, Phillis died. Her obituary ran in the *Independent Chronicle and Universal Advertiser*. It was one of the few papers to note her death.

Timeline

1761—Phillis Wheatley arrives in Boston from West Africa. She is sold as a slave to the Wheatley family.

1767—Phillis's first poem is published.

1771—Phillis joins Boston's Old South Church.

1773—Phillis is freed by the Wheatleys. The Boston Tea Party happens. Phillis's book of poetry is published. It is the first book of poetry written by an African American.

1774—Mrs. Wheatley dies.

1778—Mr. Wheatley and Mary Wheatley die. Phillis marries John Peters.

1784—Phillis Wheatley dies.

1786—Phillis's book is first printed in America.

Glossary

abandon (uh-BAN-dun) To leave without planning to come back.

culture (KUL-chur) The beliefs, practices, art, and faiths of a group of people.

debtor (DEH-tur) One who owes.

historian (hih-STOR-ee-un) Someone who studies the past.

kidnapped (KID-napt) Having been carried off by force.

memoir (MEHM-wahr) A biography or an account written by someone with personal knowledge.

publication (puhb-lih-CAY-shun) A book, magazine, or other work made available to the public.

society (soh-SY-ih-tee) A group of people with similar traditions, activities, and institutions.

Learn More

Books

Calvert, Jennifer. *Teen Trailblazers: 30 Fearless Girls Who Changed the World Before They Were 20*. New York, NY: Castle Point Books, 2018.

Doak, Robin S. *Phillis Wheatley: The Inspiring Life Story of the American Poet*. North Mankato, MN: Compass Point Books, 2017.

Harrison, Vashti. *Little Leaders: Bold Women in Black History*. New York, NY: Little, Brown and Company, 2017.

Websites

African-American Firsts: Women
biography.com/people/groups/african-american-firsts-women
Explore this collection of pioneering African American women.

Phillis Wheatley Biography
biography.com/people/phillis-wheatley-9528784
Find out more about Phillis Wheatley.

The Rise of Slavery
americanhistoryforkids.com/the-rise-of-slavery/
Learn more about slavery in America.

Primary Source Image List

Page 4: Map of Africa, drawn and engraved by John Senex, 1725.

Page 7: Ad for slave auction placed by William Yeoman, 1744, *Charleston Gazette*, Charleston, South Carolina.

Page 8: *The New-England Primer*, printed and sold in Boston, Massachusetts, 1737.

Page 9: *Brown's Family Bible*, American Edition, List of Subscribers, first published in England in 1778.

Page 10: Engraving of George Whitefield, by Elisha Gallaudet, 1774. From *Memoirs of the life of the Reverend George Whitefield*, M.A., *late chaplain to the Right Honourable the Countess of Huntingdon*.

Page 11: "On the Death of the Reverend George Whitefield, 1770," written by Phillis Wheatley, engraved in Boston, Massachusetts.

Page 13: "An Address to the Atheist," written by Phillis Wheatley in her own hand.

Page 14: Portrait of David Hume, by Allan Ramsay, oil on canvas, 1766.

Page 15: Letter from George Washington, February 28, 1776, in his own hand.

Page 17: Top: Portrait of John Hancock, c. 1765, by John Singleton Copley, oil on canvas. Bottom: Introduction to book of poetry by Phillis Wheatley, written by John Wheatley, of Boston, Massachusetts, 1772.

Page 18: *Boston Tea Party*, by W. D. Cooper, engraving, 1789.

Page 19: *The Death of General Warren at the Battle of Bunker Hill, June 17, 1775* painted in oil from memory by John Trumbull in 1786.

Primary Source Image List

Page 21: Colorized copy of *Phillis Wheatley, Negro Servant to Mr. John Wheatley, of Boston*, an engraving believed to be based on a portrait by Scipio Moorhead. The engraving was the frontispiece for *Poems on Various Subjects, Religious and Moral* by Phillis Wheatley, printed for A. Bell, Aldgate, England, 1773.

Page 22: Portrait of Phillis Wheatley, believed to be based on a print by W. E. Braxton, printed in *Revue des colonies*, Paris, France, between 1834 and 1842.

Page 24: Handwritten letter written from Phillis Wheatley to Obour Tanner, March 21, 1774.

Page 26: Phillis Wheatley newspaper obituary, *Independent Chronicle and Universal Advertiser*, December 9, 1784, Boston, Massachusetts.

Index